ZOMBIES ATE MY MOM!

MARK FASSETT

Other Books By
Mark Fassett

The Sacrifice of Mendleson Moony

A Wizard's Work
Shattered
* Fragments
* Reworked

Lords of Genova
Questioner's Shadow

* *Forthcoming*

ZOMBIES ATE MY MOM!

MARK FASSETT

RAVENSTAR PRESS
MONROE, WA

Published 2012 by Ravenstar Press
Monroe, WA
http://www.ravenstarpress.com

Trade paper edition designed by Mark Fassett
in Scribus

Electronic editions designed by Mark Fassett
using StoryBox software
http://www.markfassett.com
http://www.storyboxsoftware.com

Cover design: Mark Fassett
Image © Chrisharvey | Dreamstime.com

ISBN: 978-0615616582

For Rebecca,
and also
for throwing at a zombie
just as you turn to run.

1

Shit.

Shit, shit.

Shit shit shit.

Fucking shit.

Oh my fucking god!

That was about the extent of my vocabulary when I first realized what had happened to my mother, and what had a pretty good chance of happening to me. They ripped her apart. Those maggot infested reanimated fucks tore her limbs from her body like they were supermen pulling apart string cheese. I mean, for Christ's sake, how can the dead be so fucking strong? They're fuckin' dead!

Honestly, I wasn't even sure they were reanimated. They just looked that way to me as I backpedaled down the sidewalk before turning to run like a motherfucker away from them. I've seen all the movies, all the end of the world shit. These don't look anything like those rage infected people in *28 Days Later*. No. They look more like the things in *Dawn of the Dead*, except these fuckers, it turns out, can run. Who the fuck knew?

So, I'm going to call them zombies, and until I can find a better term, that's what they'll be.

Fuck. I'm not even sure where they came from. Mom and I were just walking down the street, right about twilight, on our way to get a take-and-bake pizza, when we saw the first one about a block down the street. I thought he was one of the drunks that came out of Harvey's Tavern down that way. He was listing pretty bad to the left as he walked toward us.

And then a couple more appeared from around the corner, and I said to my mom, "Do you think Harvey's just emptied?"

"Why would it?" she asked. "That place never closes."

We kept walking, thinking they were drunks, and that we would just walk past them. We only had another half block to go before we arrived at the pizza place. We thought we'd be fine.

That lasted all of about two minutes, until those fuckers finally noticed us and ran right at us.

I grabbed my mother's arm and tried to pull her along with me, but she stumbled and fell to the ground. She tried to get up, and then one of those pieces of shit jumped out from the bushes beside us, grabbed hold of her arm, and yanked it right off.

I crapped my pants. The zombie turned and looked at me for a moment, and I could see into its skull through an empty eye socket. The other eye blinked in an apparent attempt to move its drooping eyelid out of the way.

"Shit!"

"Shit, shit!"

And all the rest that I told you up front, and then I turned and ran. Those fuckers may be superman strong and able to run, but they weren't track stars, and they couldn't fly.

I didn't have to keep the tears back. They wouldn't come at all. Don't get me wrong. I loved my mom, but in that moment, with zombies bearing down on me and my shorts full of yesterday's breakfast, I didn't have time to think about how my mother had died, or that she was even dead.

I looked over my shoulder once, and the zombies had fallen off, returning to chow on my mom.

I ran back to my apartment, which my mom had been visiting. It's only about three blocks away from the pizza place. I ran up the stairs, fumbled my keys out of my pocket, somehow managed to unlock the door, and jumped inside, locking the door behind me.

I grabbed the phone and dialed 911. I know, you're asking why I didn't just dial 911 on my cell as I was running. The answer is that I hate those fucking things. People always calling you, texting you, invading your life at inconvenient times. So I leave the one I have at home as often as I can get away with it. I have it for work reasons. When I don't want to be called by my work, I leave it at home. It's not like you can anticipate a zombie attack every fucking day.

Fucking 911 gave me a busy signal. "Fuck!"

Andrea, I thought. *I'll call Andrea.* Her

number gave me a busy signal, too. “What the fuck?”

I was freaked out before, but as I dialed numbers and got busy signals, my efforts grew more and more frantic until I eventually threw the phone across the room and smashed my beer bottle collection. “God fucking dammit!”

Think, think! I peeked out through the blinds and didn’t see anything. Of course, it had grown darker, and those things didn’t exactly carry flashlights or wear glow sticks.

I had time. Time to get cleaned up and change my pants.

What a fucking mess.

Once that was done and I’d tossed it all in the trash—I’m not cleaning that up—and tied off the trashbag, the whole fucking nightmare hit me like a punch in the chest. My mom, dead. Cause of death—zombies.

Unless she is a zombie now.

Fuck. That hurts. They pulled her apart. I don’t think there’s any chance she became one of them.

“What the hell do I do, now?” I asked no one in particular.

"You could try 911 again, dumbass," I answered myself.

I looked over to where the hurled phone had tumbled through the beer bottles and wondered if there was any chance it had survived. Some of my favorite bottles hadn't.

Nothing for it, though. I had to go check it out.

It was cracked, right along the earpiece, but I thought it should still work. I put it up to my ear, pressed the talk button, but it was dead. I threw it at a still standing pile of bottles and knocked them over, too.

Then I spotted my cell sitting on my desk next to the computer. I gave in, and decided I'd have to see if the piece of shit worked. I dialed 911, and again got a busy signal.

"Useless." I almost tossed the cell, too, and thought better of it.

I tried Andrea again. No dice, only this time, instead of a busy signal, I got an automated message that the call couldn't go through. Right about now, I found myself wishing I had a radio or a TV, but who has those anymore? I watch all the shows I want for free online.

I must not have been thinking straight. In my panic, I'd reverted to what I'd grown up with.

I sat down at my computer and waited the three seconds for it to resume from sleep mode. I love solid state disk drives. So much speed. When it came up, I checked CNN first thing, in case maybe the zombie apocalypse was upon us. I don't know why I even bothered. They didn't even have an alert up or anything. Either it wasn't national, or they were ass slow as always, or they'd all been eaten. I voted for number two.

And then Twitter chimed. And chimed again. I brought it up, and damn if Twitter hadn't just blown up. Everyone was talking about zombies. Fuck. Thank God for the internet.

I started typing.

@PsychoAndrea You OK? My Mom's de...

The power went out. Black as shit.

I peeked out the window through the blinds to see if the building across the street had power, but their place was dark, too. At least the outage wasn't local. I breathed a sigh of relief as I decided that the zombies hadn't followed me home.

But then I saw some movement in the parking

lot, a shadow or something. In the dark, I didn't know where the light came from to give me that glimpse, but I didn't care. One of those fucking things was in my parking lot.

Now, I guess I should describe my apartment. It's not one of those huge apartment complexes that you see all over the place. No, it's a late sixties rambler that the owner decided to convert into apartments. The place is a dive, but the neighbors are cool most of the time. I don't have to worry about blasting music or drinking and getting too loud, because they're doing it all the time themselves, when they're not high on pot.

I stumbled back to my computer and reached for the tiny LED flashlight I kept there. It wouldn't give off a lot of light, but it would help me find something to use against those things. I had no illusion that I would survive the night in this place if I didn't take steps. It's not like the place had bullet proof glass for windows and a bank vault door in the entryway.

"Fuck you!" I heard through my wall. My neighbor, Danny.

He followed it up with a couple of shots from his gun, loud explosions, a thump against the wall.

My heart raced.

"Danny!" I yelled through the wall. "You all right?"

"Fuuuck!" Another shot, this one zinged past my ear.

No, Danny wasn't all right, and he had the only gun in the place.

I flipped my flashlight on and looked around my place while the yelling and thumping continued next door.

Nothing. Broken beer bottles wouldn't do a thing against those creatures. I didn't own any weapons, or even many tools beyond the screwdrivers I used to work on my computers. What I wouldn't give for a BFG.

Then I shined the light into the corner, and I saw two of those metal rails that you screw to the wall to hold up bookshelves.

"Better than nothing."

I grabbed one of them, searched for my car keys in my pocket until I realized that they were in the pocket of the pants I'd soiled. Getting them out of that bag wasn't pleasant.

The noise next door stopped.

"Time to go," I said in a whisper. After I said it, I wished I'd kept my mouth shut. I had no idea if these things tracked by sight or smell or sound, and I knew one had to be next door.

And, since I hadn't heard anything else from Danny, I had to assume he was dead, too. At that moment, I realized that my other neighbor's dogs, a pair of rottweilers, should have been barking their heads off, but they were silent. If I stayed any longer, I'd be zombie food.

I peeked out the window again and didn't see anything move. Maybe it was still eating Danny. I hoped there was only the one.

I stuck the flashlight in my pocket, put the bookshelf rail in one hand, my car keys in the other. I turned the knob, then pulled the door open just a touch so I could look through the crack. Nothing. I let out a sigh of relief. I'd half expected one of the maggot-ridden to be standing right on the step.

I started to step out when I heard glass shatter behind me.

Something smashed through my front window. Something. A fucking zombie smashed through my window. It tripped itself up on the obsolete CD rack I'd left there, and fell head first into the open crappy-pants bag.

I screamed, and then ran out the door.

I could see it through the window, now that it was inside, and I was outside. It was just starting to stand.

How can I see? I looked up. Starlight. I hadn't seen starlight in months. The power was out fucking everywhere.

I ran for my car, a beat up old piece of shit Honda Civic. When I got to its door, I fumbled the keys to the ground in my haste to get the door unlocked. The thought that ran through my head? *God dammit this kind of shit is only fucking supposed to happen in the movies!*

I looked back into my apartment and saw that the zombie—I'll call him Joe because I fucking hate the name Joe—had righted himself and had turned to come back through the now glassless window.

"Fuck!"

That's what Danny said right before he died, I thought.

I bent down and felt around the ground for my

keys with my free hand while I kept my eye on Joe. Gravel, gravel. A stick. *Where the fuck are my keys?*

Joe's left leg stepped out of my apartment and into the the flowerbed full of weeds underneath it.

I reached farther under the car, and my fingers found a piece of metal. The keyring. I hooked it with my index finger and pulled it out.

I manipulated the keys with my fingers, while keeping my eyes on Joe, until I found the plastic shell of my car key. I'd always hated the plastic shells they stuck on the keys, but if anyone had asked me at that moment, I would have sung the praises of plastic.

I jammed the key in the door as Joe cleared the window sill and started an off center jog toward me.

I gave up on the key for the moment and prepared to take on Joe. I couldn't let him get near me or he'd rip me apart, so I held that steel rail out in front of me, pointed straight at the fucker.

According to most of the movies, you kill a zombie with a blow to the head. "Is that how you die, Joe?" I asked. Of course, there was that other movie series where you had to cremate them or something. If I had to do that, I was fucked. Of course, I remembered that didn't turn out so well, either.

I decided, in the split second I had, to try for the head.

As Joe drew close to me, I could hear him grunting with the effort of movement.

I stabbed out with the rail, aiming where I thought his head would be.

Fuck! The rail stopped dead. I'd hit Joe in the head, but struck bone. Joe slowed for a moment, giving me a chance.

I backed up, ran around the car to try to give myself a little more time.

Joe followed me.

"Come on, you fucker!" I yelled at him.

As Joe followed me around the back of the car to the passenger side, I moved toward the front of the car and around it, until I found myself at the driver side door again.

Unfortunately, Joe didn't follow my plan. He started climbing over the car. A hand broke through the passenger window, and glass rained all over the seat within. Joe got a foot up, and then levered himself up on the roof, with his head toward me, a perfect target.

I jammed the end of the rail at his face over the roof of the car. This time, I struck paydirt—or pay-brains. The rail slipped right into Joe's eye-socket.

Joe screamed a scream that I would have thought might come from a dying cat or something. It wasn't human. And then Joe went limp on the roof of my car.

"Fucker! Fuck you!" I yelled.

I pulled the key from the car door, got in, and started the car.

As soon as the engine turned over, I put the piece of crap into reverse and hit the gas.

Joe slid down the window and off the hood, leaving streaks of some dark goo as he went. I had left the bookshelf rail embedded in his head, and it scraped my hood as it went with Joe. For a brief moment, I thought about retrieving it, but I decided Joe could keep it. I didn't want zombie goo on my seats.

I stopped the car, put it in drive, spun the wheel, and punched the gas.

A couple quick bumps as the wheels rolled over Joe's dead body, and I found myself on the road, unsure of my destination.

I missed my mom, already.

I think I should say something about my mom. She was the best. I could count on her for anything, and I often did. Short on food? Mom says, “I’ll make dinner for you.” Short on cash? “Here’s some money to get you through.” Have a problem at work? She’d listen to me talk for hours about those asshats I work with, even though she probably didn’t understand a quarter of what I said.

She was always there.

Her loss hit me right then, as I was driving away from an apartment I suspected I would never see again. I couldn’t ask her for help, for an idea, or for anything else.

“God damned cock sucking mother fucking

zombies!" I yelled as I pounded the steering wheel until my hand hurt. I felt tears roll down my cheeks, and it quickly grew harder to see, but I kept driving. It seemed to me that pulling over could be a craptastic idea.

Besides, there weren't that many cars on the road.

I wiped at my eyes until I could see again, and tried to reign in the tears. "You can fucking cry later," I told myself, but I wasn't even listening. I was searching the road for any sign of life.

I saw nothing at first. Just a bunch of parked cars. The road itself was empty. I wondered where everyone went. They had to know by now. The street I was driving down, while not a freeway, never lacked for traffic.

Then I saw someone, a shadow really, standing on the side of the road. I slowed the car a bit and rolled down my window. I'm not stupid enough to have stopped. Don't forget, I've seen all the movies. This was exactly the part of the movie where the dumbass pulls over to ask a question, only to have the zombie leap through the window and kill him.

I'm not *that* dumbass.

"Hey," I called.

I didn't hear an answer, but in the dark, I thought I saw the person turn to look at me.

"Hey, where is everyone?" I know it was a stupid question, but it was the best I had at the time. I probably should have spent my first words telling him to watch out for zombies, but as it turned out, I would have been too late, anyway.

The thing rushed my car.

Its jaw hung at an odd angle. It ran without a limp. Fuck.

I stepped hard on the gas. I already had one broken window. I didn't want another. The car accelerated, a little slow as I hadn't given it a tune-up in who knows how long. The zombie raced toward me, and then the car finally realized I wanted it to go. It leaped forward just at the moment the zombie reached out for my window.

The zombie slammed into the rear quarter-panel. I looked in my mirror, and watched it tumble away in the darkness.

"Yeah, bitch!" My heart pounded in my chest, and the encounter decided me.

I had to find a weapon, something better than a bookshelf rail. I couldn't shoot a gun for shit, hadn't shot one since since my dad took me to the range and had me shoot his .22. For whatever reason, I was afraid of it, and I only managed to hit the target once.

It would be nice to be able to shoot like the actors in zombie movies. These people who can't hit a thing, as soon as they're told to shoot for the head, every bullet manages to take out a zombie. I always laughed at how unrealistic that kind of thing was, but then, zombies weren't exactly a real sort of scenario. Who the fuck knew?

Anyway, I knew where I could get the kind of weapons I needed. All it meant was that I'd have to put off getting Andrea for another twenty minutes. It meant I would have to face my dad.

Fuck. It meant I would have to tell Dad about Mom.

When I got to the end of the street, I could turn left to go to Andrea's, or turn right to head to my dad's. I almost turned left. I needed to know if she was all right.

I even flicked my blinker on to go that way,

until I saw a woman running down the street from that direction. She was looking behind her, where three nightmares ran after her. If she had been looking where she was going, she might have seen the big fucker that jumped out from the bushes and knocked her to the ground before tearing into her. She screamed out for help, a piercing wail that bounced off a retaining wall and entered through my broken window.

I spun my wheel to the right and put as much distance between me and them as I could.

So my dad lives across town. Lynnwood is not a large city. It's a city built around shopping, as far as I can tell. Nearly every building, if it isn't residential, serves a retail purpose. Normally, I can get to his place in about ten minutes, but that way takes me under the freeway in one of the busiest parts of town.

The freeway will take you south to Seattle, or north to Everett, two places I knew I wouldn't want to go if the world had just become as fucked as Twitter said it had. More people meant more zombies. More zombies mean more people trying to get out on the freeway. But, I thought I'd at least take a look. Maybe I'd get lucky.

The lights of a car appeared from around the bend in front of me. Another live person. I let out a breath I hadn't known I'd been holding. The car's lights flashed as it came toward me. The universal acknowledgment of bad shit up ahead, usually a cop waiting for speeders.

The car raced past me.

A glow showed itself around the bend, and I thought for a moment the power was on, but dread filled me. I knew I was coming up on the freeway underpass, and with the way that guy was flashing his lights, it occurred to me that going this way might be a shit idea.

It was the fastest way to my dad's place, though. I slowed down, and crept around the bend, expecting to run into something.

The road straightened out right at the top of the hill that lead to the freeway underpass, and what I saw as I looked down on it, and across the huge retail complex the city had become, caused me to slam on my breaks. I was not lucky.

The glow I had seen came from the headlights of thousands of cars stuck on the freeway, the on-ramps, and the underpass, and all roads leading to it, mixed with the dancing orange light of a city on fire.

There were shadows, people, running among the unmoving cars, and rotten meat sacks chased them all.

I sat and watched for long moments in disbelief. I had known, of course, from Twitter, that shit was bad everywhere, and I've seen shots like this in movies, but images on a screen don't compare to the magnitude of seeing it happen in front of your own eyes.

In those moments of watching the spectacle, I found myself wanting to shut down, to sit in my car and cry. I wanted to cry for my mom, for the craptastic life I had been living, for the knowledge that I'd never get to eat fish and chips again. And tears did come. My eyes blurred with them, and I blinked them away, wiped at my eyes to clear them, but the tears wouldn't stop.

My cell phone rang.

Where was it?

It had fallen off the seat. I scrambled around, digging through the piles of fast food garbage in the passenger seat foot area. I found it right before it would have gone to voice mail.

I pressed talk and held it to my ear without even looking at the number.

"Hello?" I asked.

"Brad?" It was Andrea. I relaxed at the sound of her voice. I still couldn't quite stop the tears, though.

"Andrea," I said. "Are you all right?"

"Yeah, yeah. I'm okay. Where are you? I've been trying to call you since two, but the lines were all jammed." I had expected to hear panic in her voice, but heard relief instead.

I couldn't, at that moment, tell her where I'd been. I didn't want to think about my mom while Andrea was on the phone. "I'm on my way to my dad's," I said.

She swallowed some air. "Don't go," she said. "Don't go anywhere near the freeway. The radio says zombies are crawling all over it."

"I know."

"You know?"

"I'm looking right at it. The city is burning."

"Get out of there!" I had to pull the phone away from my ear. It fucking hurt.

"Calm down," I said. "I'm at the top of the hill.

I'm not fucking going down there. How's your apartment? Are you safe?"

I'd always hated that her apartment was on the top floor. Too many fucking stairs. Now, though, that might be the best thing about it. No access through the windows, as long as the zombie motherfuckers couldn't scale the wall.

"Yeah, the door is shut and locked."

The other good thing about her apartment. The front doors were heavy steel. I didn't think a zombie could get through them.

"Then stay there. I'm going to my dad's to get some weapons, then I'll come get you and we'll find a safe place to ride this out."

"No, come get me now."

There was no fucking way I was taking her to my dad's. "No, your place is far safer. Just stay there. Put something heavy in front of the door, just in case. I'll be there as soon as I can."

"But..."

"No," I said. "You don't have any idea what it's like out here. I'm not..."

A shadow flitted across the road ahead of me, far too close for me to be happy about it.

“Brad?”

Another shadow followed it.

“Oh, fuck. Stay there, Andrea.”

I dropped the phone onto the seat, slammed the car into reverse, and hit the gas.

The car ran into something, shattering the rear window, but it didn’t stop the car. I turned around to look, and found my rear window had been replaced by the upper body of a dead man. He was still moving, though.

I pushed the speed up as far as I could while in reverse. It’s not as easy as movies make it look.

I smashed on the breaks. The wheels broke loose from the pavement, and the next thing I knew, I was spinning toward the side of the road.

When shit happens that fast, you hear about people talking how time slows down. Not for me. The car spun like crazy, and then it stopped, and I couldn’t have told you how it happened if I hadn’t looked down and found the wheels right up against the curb.

The jolt, as it happened, did do one thing. My dinner patron seemed to have left the premises.

As luck would have it, I was facing away from

the freeway, and the car was still running. I heard a noise behind me, outside of the car. I didn't bother to look. I hit the gas and drove off.

It didn't take long to figure out that the collision with the curb had put at least one of the wheels out of alignment. I began to wonder if I'd make it to my dad's in this car. Two busted windows now, wheels out of alignment. I'm just damned lucky I didn't break one of them off.

"Fuck!" I looked upward, not that I believed in God before then, but I really felt like I needed some help, now. "Please, don't cause a wheel to fall off just because I thought I'd gotten lucky!"

I hate it when I think those things, too. Just when something goes right, and I get excited about it, I think about something bad that could have happened and didn't. Inevitably, I find myself dealing with said problem moments later.

"Focus, dumbass," I said. "Get to your dad's, grab a sword or three, guns for Andrea, and get over to her place."

I passed the road to my apartment. The zombies that had been there were gone. A lump of something lay off to the left. I tried not to look at it as I passed.

And then I found myself on the back roads, circling the city of fire.

While I drove, I pondered how the infection, it's always an infection, spread so far, so fast. I laughed to myself. The movies always start out with at least one of the main characters being completely oblivious to what was going on. I had never imagined that would be me, but somehow, I'd avoided all mentions of it until my mom and I encountered those fuckers.

I knew how I'd avoided it, too. My mom and I had spent the whole day together, talking, reminiscing, and planning. I'd let slip that I was planning to ask Andrea to marry me, and my mom got all excited. She really liked Andrea, I think, or maybe she liked the idea of Andrea. My mom hated the place I lived. The looks she gave it every time she came over, if she had lasers in her eyes, she would have burned the place down.

So my mom had come over to help me plan the perfect way to ask Andrea.

Of course, that's all fucked now, and I can't ever tell Andrea that my mom died today because she'd come over to help me plan "the question".

By the time I hit Maple Road, which would lead me over I-5, the wobbly wheel had grown more resistant to the idea of rolling straight. It was going to come off, just a matter of time. Of course, I had run over two more zombies, one of which had gone under that wheel. I'm sure that hadn't helped.

I didn't bother to count the empty cars that I had passed, nor did I stop to check them out. The zombies that had precipitated their emptiness were nearly always still hanging around, eating the previous owner. Without a weapon, I didn't have a chance.

I just had to pray the car would get me to my dad's, where I could probably borrow one of his tanks (a euphemism for really big, gas-guzzling, SUV). One of them happened to be called an "Armada", which I used to find really amusing as the name of a vehicle, since an armada generally consists of multiple vehicles. Of course, right then, I would have welcomed an armada with me.

I came upon the bridge that crossed over I-5; it turned out to be mercifully clear. I had worried that it would be clogged with people looking down at the freeway below.

I slowed down a bit as I crossed. I couldn't get a good look at the freeway right below me, but lights stretched as far as I could see in either direction on both sides of the freeway. Shadows slid in and out among them.

I looked to my left and could just make out Alderwood mall over the tops of some trees. I knew it was likely too late for the mall to be open, but there were lights on, and the parking lot was packed with cars. It was far enough away that I couldn't tell if there were people or zombies outside of the shopping complex, but I'm not dumb. Cars equal people equal zombies.

I chuckled as I put my foot into the gas a bit more. The zombie movies with empty malls. Great place to go. Apparently, everyone else thought so, too.

The road wound under 525, before it came to an intersection. Another place I was worried I'd get stuck, but except for a couple of stiffs and an overturned mini-van resting in the other lane, it was free of obstacles.

I managed to avoid the stiffs without doing more damage to my wobbly wheel and navigated my way up into the housing development on the other side.

I expected to see a lot of damage, houses burning, that kind of shit. Mostly, though, the homes looked lifeless and empty. Driveways were free of cars, the streets free of people and zombies. If I hadn't just experienced all that I had, I might have thought it was a normal night but for the lack of power.

I knew where they all were, and didn't really want to admit it. They'd all tried to get out of town, and they were now all zombie food, if they weren't zombies themselves. That's one thing I wasn't really sure of yet. Was this zombie apocalypse because of a contagion, or was it the supernatural kind that only makes sense in movies, and only then if you completely ignore anything resembling science? Did people who get bit turn into zombies? The way these things pulled people apart, I couldn't imagine it.

As I pulled up to the last turn I would have to make to reach my dad's house, I was surprised the wobbly wheel was still on the car. The ride had grown so rough, I'd bitten my tongue more than a few times until I learned to keep my teeth clamped together.

I turned, and the wheel fell off. The front left corner of the car dug into the pavement and came to a stop. My head snapped forward a bit, causing my neck to ache, but I hadn't been driving that fast. The airbags didn't deploy, but the car shut down. The lights still lit up an area of the road that extended just to the front lawn of the house across the street.

I looked out through the windows and didn't see anything moving. I got out of the car and slammed the door shut. "Cocksucking car," I said. The echo of the two noises, the slammed door and my epithet, reverberated among the house momentarily. When it was done, it left the street silent.

My dad's house was at the end of the street, looming over a cul-de-sac. When he'd built it, he'd purchased two of the plots of land to build it on. I don't know how he managed to get the city to let him bypass the zoning laws, but he did. My dad may be an asshole, but he's an influential asshole.

The street was dark. There were enough trees around and among the houses that they blocked a lot of the starlight. I could have kicked myself. I either had to walk or run the quarter mile down the street in the near dark, or I had to go back into the car and get my flashlight out of the glove-box. I should have thought of that in the first place.

I walked around the car to the broken passenger side window. I scanned the area around me, and couldn't see anything. The street was still silent, but for my footsteps.

I reached in, popped the glove-box open, and grabbed my flashlight. Unfortunately, it wasn't one of those big metal flashlights that could be used as a weapon. Nope. I had to have a small, plastic flashlight. For weapons, I'd have to look elsewhere. Especially since I'd left the bookshelf rail stuck in Joe's head.

I flicked it on. It still worked.

I heard footsteps behind me, running. I turned around and shined the flashlight on it. The fucker's head exploded and the body skidded to a stop in front of me, and then I heard the crack of a rifle from behind me.

Fuck. My dad must be having some sort of fun. I may not be able to shoot for shit, but my dad. Damn. He was a sniper in the Gulf War back in the 90's, so he says. I'm not sure whether I can believe that, but he took out that zombie at a quarter of a mile.

The flashlight came up a little more, and off in the distance, I saw more zombies stumbling down the street. This time, they wouldn't have my mom to eat.

I turned to run, and my phone rang. In the fucking car. Fuck!

I flashed my light on the zombies again. I had time, if I hurried. Another zombie dropped, another crack from the rifle.

I flashed the light in the car, the phone was on the floor again. Fuck.

I pulled open the door, reached in, grabbed the phone, and stood back up. My flashlight lit up a zombie, its mouth wide open in a silent scream, not six feet from me.

It dropped, its head exploding like the others. I bet my fucking dad would love me to just stand here and shine my flashlight on them.

Fuck him. I wasn't staying.

Cell phone in one hand, flashlight in the other,

I ran as hard as I could toward my dad's house. After my earlier run to save my life from my mom's attackers, I pretty quickly found out I was gassed. I hadn't eaten anything, and the earlier run had used up what was left. My chest started to hurt and my legs began to ache after I'd covered about half the distance to the house. Made me wish I'd had a better diet and a bit more exercise. Seems like the character Columbus from *Zombieland* had it right. Cardio is important.

I had to slow down to catch my breath. I flashed the light behind me, and I had put some distance on them, but I couldn't stop.

I heard my dad's voice yell out, "Keep running!"

I can do this, I thought to myself. *Just two more football fields.*

Right. Like I'd run even that far since high-school, and now, I'd done it twice in the same day.

But I picked up my pace, knowing that the silent, running mob was not far behind me, and safety, such as it was, lay ahead of me.

I felt dead when I finally reached the gate to

my dad's property. He was there to open the side door for me, and I stumbled through and fell to the ground, gasping for air. The door clanked shut behind me.

I guess I forgot to mention. My dad is fucking paranoid. Rich, and paranoid. Makes for fun times. His whole property is fenced with iron bars. It has cameras all along the perimeter. He has a generator or three, too, but for some reason, they weren't running. He had all his lights off.

He reached down and shut my flashlight off.

"The light attracts them," he said.

Fucking great.

3

I mentioned my dad's place is like a small fortress. What surprised me, once I stood up, was how many people were standing around inside the fence with him. It looked like nearly the whole fucking neighborhood. I'd always thought my dad was a bit of an asshole. He kept people away for the most part. To see his courtyard filled with people was kind of amazing.

"You're not bit, are you, Brad?" my dad asked.

I shook my head.

"Alright," he said, grabbing my arm. I swear he had more strength in his hand than I had in my whole body. He always had. "Chuck," he said, "take care of those assholes out there. I need to talk to my boy."

A man in the crowd said, “Yup.” I didn’t get a good look at him in the dark, but he unslung his rifle.

I turned and looked at the fence. I hadn’t noticed with all my heavy breathing, but the zombies had come right up to the fence, and were trying to get in. They couldn’t get more than hands and arms through, but it creeped me out. I didn’t really feel safe. They didn’t moan, like I thought they should, like they did in the movies, but you could hear their bodies sliding up against each other and against the fence.

Chuck walked up to the fence, just out of arm’s reach, put his rifle to his shoulder, sighted between the bars, and put a bullet through a zombie’s head. It fell to the ground and another took its place. There were a lot of fucking zombies out there.

“Come on,” my dad said to me and pulled me along with him.

Another shot rang out behind me. My ears were ringing.

The inside of the house was lit. Of course—blackout shades on the windows.

The house was packed with people, sitting and standing in every corner of the place. It gave me a new appreciation for my dad. "I can't believe you let all these people in," I said.

He said nothing, only led me through them to the back of his house and his office. The doors were shut. A half dozen men and women sat to either side of the doors.

"Have you eaten?" he asked me as he fumbled in his pocket for a keyring.

"Not since lunch."

"Sarah," he said to one of the women as he stuck the key in the lock and twisted it. "Could you get a plate of food for my son and bring it here?"

Sarah stood up. She was tall, six feet, at least, with dark eyes and a tan that said she vacationed somewhere it didn't rain. "Anything in particular?" She was looking at me.

"Just tell Alicia to serve him up," my dad said for me.

Alicia. My step-mom. My knees suddenly felt weak. Why the fuck was she still alive? I don't really harbor any ill will toward her. It's not her fault my parents split up, but if one of them had to die, why did it have to be my mom and not her?

I blinked my eyes shut. I didn't want to cry again, not in front of my dad and these people.

The door opened, and I squeezed past my dad and into the room. I went right to a chair he kept in the corner, sat down, and stared up at the ceiling, all the while trying to breathe slowly, evenly, and deeply. I needed to calm myself. I couldn't let my dad see me break down. I didn't want him to look at me like he'd always looked at me. Like he'd looked at me since that day at the rifle range where I had disappointed him.

I heard the door shut, and my dad crossed the room to sit in his chair behind the war room desk. That's what he'd called this room ever since he built the house. The war room. It was fitting. He kept most of his weapons in this room, except for the guns he had stashed throughout the rest of the house—just in case.

"I can tell by your face," he said, some of the commanding tone missing from his voice, "that your mother is dead."

"They tore her apart," I said, and then the tears came out anyway.

I sobbed for a minute or two, and nothing else

was said between us. When I finally got it under control enough to look up, I saw him with his head in his arms on the desk. His body was shaking. He wasn't making any noise. He couldn't allow that to happen, but he was crying. I had never seen that before.

"Dad?" I said.

He looked up. Tears stained his cheeks.

Someone knocked on the door.

"Get that, will you," he said, and turned away.

I went to the door and opened it up a bit. The woman, Sarah, had a plate of something hot, chicken, I think, mixed with noodles. It smelled delicious. I'm glad it wasn't pizza.

She passed the plate to me through the slightly open door, and followed it with a glass of water.

"Thanks," I said, then nudged the door shut with my foot.

I took the food back to my chair and started eating. It was delicious. As much as I wanted to hate Alicia for being alive at that moment, she was a good cook.

My dad turned around. He'd composed

himself. His rigid jaw was set, his eyes focused. Maybe the whole Gulf War sniper story was true.

"Tell me the story," he said.

In between bites, I related what had happened. He sat there and listened to me without interrupting. It actually started to worry me that he wasn't reacting at all. I mean, I already blamed myself for what had happened. Why didn't I do this? Why not that? But it had happened so fast. I expected my dad to lecture me on situational awareness or some other shit that he'd always tried to drill into me. I expected him to blame me for Mom's death.

I finished telling him about my mom, and he nodded and said, "Go on."

Fuck. He wanted to hear the rest. So I told him.

Once I'd finished, he steepled his hands just like school principals you see in movies, and then he said the unexpected. "I don't know what you could have done for your mom. Even if you had a weapon, the way you shoot, you would have just as likely shot her as those assholes."

He paused for a moment, staring at me. "Obviously, you made some mistakes. You should have checked the news before you went out, but then—nobody expects this kind of shit to come down. You did a damned fine job getting over here. A fucking bookshelf rail? That's impressive. I'd always thought you were afraid of fighting, but a bookshelf rail?"

He chuckled a sort of dark, hurt, chuckle. He still wanted to cry.

"You know, I loved your mom. I know I was a shitty husband to her, I know I didn't pay her enough attention. We just grew apart. If only..."

"Look, Dad, I know."

He sniffed once, and then sat straight up. Back to Major Dad. "Well, I'm glad you're here. We can use you."

"Why are all these people here," I asked. "I would have thought you would keep everybody out."

"I served our country, son. My job was to protect the innocent against evil, and I did it. I still do it. That's what you and your mom never understood. I wasn't preparing just for me, but for our friends, our neighbors. I've got a ton of storage downstairs, even more than you know. When the first news reports hit this morning, I knew something was fucked up. I had Alicia call our neighbors, our friends, told them to come here."

"She didn't call me."

A look of concern crossed his face. "She didn't? She told me she couldn't reach you, that it went straight to voice mail."

And then it dawned on me. My cell phone had been off.

My cell phone.

I reached into my pocket where I had stuffed my phone and pulled it out. Someone had been calling me right as I was leaving my car. Andrea. '1 Missed Call'. Fuck!

"I had it turned off," I said as I frantically opened my phone to see who had called. It was Andrea.

I hit send and put it to my ear. It rang, once, twice. She picked up.

"Brad, your alive!"

"Yes, you're safe?" I asked.

"For now. There's something pushing at the door, trying to get in, but I've got all my furniture pushed in front of it. What happened?"

"Long story. But I'm at my dad's. I'll be on my way in a little bit." If I could convince my dad to let me borrow one of the tanks.

"Okay," she said. "I'm scared."

"Me too," I said. "Just keep that door blocked, and I'll be right over."

"I love you," she said.

"I love you too."

And then I hung up. I didn't want to waste time going back and forth on one of those calls where you can't end it because no one wants to be the one to hang up first.

"And where do you think you're going?" my dad asked.

"Andrea, she's barricaded in her apartment. I need to get her out."

"Who is Andrea?"

When I told my dad about my mom, I left out the part of the story explaining why I was with my mom. It had seemed irrelevant at the time.

I cringed inside. "My girlfriend," I said.

"A girlfriend?" he asked. "Why haven't I heard about her before?"

I didn't want to tell him the truth, which was that I was afraid of his reaction. I didn't think he'd be upset, I just thought he would be indifferent. So I said, "We haven't talked much." Hey, it was a truth.

He looked around the room a bit like he was taking inventory. He certainly had an inventory. Rifles, semi-automatics, pistols, shotguns. A hundred weapons or more, most of which I couldn't name.

Weapons I could name? Rail gun. Flame thrower. BFG. Laser. Grenade Launcher. Pick a video game, and I could probably name some guns in it. Give me a mouse and a keyboard, and I can hit any damned target you want me to.

"So why did you come here? Why aren't you on your way to her right now?"

The question surprised me. "Weapons, dad. I don't have any weapons."

"You can't shoot for shit."

"I can swing a bookshelf rail. I bet a sword would work better."

"Looks like you need a vehicle, too."

I nodded.

My dad got up from behind his desk and went to the door. He stuck his head outside, and I heard him ask someone to get Alicia and Chuck.

He shut the door, and turned to face me.

"Where does she live?"

"Apartments on the other side of the freeway," I said.

He grunted. "Bound to be crawling with those assholes. What kind of apartments?"

"A typical building, three floors. She's on the third."

"Tough for them to get in, but tough for us, too."

My dad went to the wall and started pulling guns down, one after another. Looked like a couple rifles, a shotgun, and some other badass looking thing. He set them on his desk.

"Can she shoot?"

"Who?"

"Your girlfriend."

"I haven't a clue."

He looked at me like I was an idiot. "Well," he said, "call her and find out."

He started rummaging through his cabinets, pulling out boxes and boxes of ammunition.

I dialed Andrea up, and after a couple rings, she answered. I was surprised the cell network was still working. Maybe there were fewer live people trying to call.

"Brad?"

"Hey, how are you doing?"

"I'm OK." She didn't sound OK. She sounded scared. I heard a thump come through the receiver.

"What was that?"

"They're still outside, pounding on the door."

"Alright. My dad wants to know if you can shoot."

"What? Of course I can shoot. My dad used to take me out to the range every weekend."

The things you don't find out about your girlfriend until the zombie apocalypse hits.

"She can shoot," I told my dad.

"Good, give me the phone."

I handed it to him.

He pointed to the wall that held his swords. "Go find one you like, or two or three."

"Hello, Andrea?"

I walked over to the wall and started looking at them, while keeping an ear on my dad's half of the conversation. He had all sorts of different swords from European styles to Japanese.

I tried to figure out what I wanted. Something not so heavy that it would tire me out, but something heavy enough to cut through a neck, and something with a point that would slip through eye sockets.

"You have a gun there?"

I reached out and picked a katana off the wall. All the dang pulp movies were in my head.

"That's a shame. Well, conserve the ammo, and shoot them in the head. Anywhere else and you're just wasting bullets."

So, not only can she shoot, but she has a gun. It started to make me worry about why she chose the PsychoAndrea nick.

The katana felt good in my hand, but it didn't have a point on it that I thought would get into the brain very easily. I'd keep it though. I could at least use it for cutting off heads.

The door opened, and Alicia slipped into the room, followed by Chuck. Now that I could see Chuck, I had a good guess that he was one of my dad's old war buddies. He was in good shape, his eyes were sharp, and his hair was shaved down where he wasn't sporting male pattern baldness.

Alicia, she was another story. She was younger than my mom, but not so young that you'd think my dad was robbing the cradle. When he met her, she had been a bit soft, though not fat by any means. Now, though, her arms had more muscle on them than mine, and she was packing a rather large pistol at her hip. It had been two years, I think, since I'd seen her, and those years had been good to her.

I turned back to the wall and saw what I was looking for. A rapier. Thin, light, probably wouldn't get stuck in an eye socket. I hoped my LARP experience would help out.

"Alright, honey, hang tough. We'll be there in a bit to get you out."

My dad hung up the phone.

Honey? I couldn't believe my ears. He handed the phone back to me and appraised my sword choices.

"You think you can be accurate enough with that thing?" he asked, indicating the rapier.

"I hope so."

"Me too. At least you won't be fighting an armed opponent."

Alicia stepped in. "Where are you going?"

"Brad and I are going to get his girlfriend."

She looked at me and smiled. “You’ve got a girlfriend? It’s about time,” she said.

I smiled back, not knowing exactly how to respond to this woman who was now the only mom I had left.

“Alicia,” my dad said. “I want you and Chuck to hold this place. You’re in charge, but let Chuck handle the defenses. If anything goes wrong, get everyone down to the basement and make sure you don’t let in anyone that’s been bit.”

“Do you really think it’s contagious?” I asked.

“Who knows, but I’ve seen those movies, too. I don’t want to risk it.”

My dad turned back to Alicia, “And make sure you keep your ear on the radios. If there’s anyone talking, try to find out where evac centers are.”

“When will you be back?” Alicia asked.

“If all goes well, I’d say an hour.”

She stepped up to my dad and put her arms around him. This part always used to bother me, but for some reason, it didn’t that night. “Do you have to go?” she asked.

“The girl is in danger,” my dad said, pulling Alicia close. “The kid’s mom is dead. He doesn’t need to lose the girl, too, if we can help it.”

She turned to look at me with a look that said she empathized. “Well, then,” she said, “you’d better hurry.”

4

I followed my dad out to the garage where he had his tanks. Only, I hadn't been in his garage in a while. He had the Armada still, and a Range Rover, but sitting behind those, he had another vehicle that loomed over them both.

"Where the hell did you get a surplus Humvee?" I asked.

He smiled. "Connections," he said. Of course, he always says connections. For all I know, there's a surplus yard where you can buy this shit for cheap. "They'd removed the weapons mount, but Chuck and I worked up a replacement. I figure you'll drive. If you got that piece of shit car of yours this far, you can probably get this thing to your girlfriend's." He handed a set of keys to me.

I'd never driven anything quite this big before, but it wasn't like it was a big rig, either. I could drive it.

I opened the door and climbed in. Dad climbed in after me, and moved back toward the weapon mount.

"Don't turn on the lights right away. We don't want the zombies to follow them to the gate."

"Right."

I heard the crack of a rifle. Chuck must already be clearing the way.

I looked up, found a garage door opener, and laughed. It seemed strange to have a garage door opener in this thing. I pressed it, and the door rolled up in front of us.

I stuck the key in, turned it, and the thing started right up. The vibrations of the motor rumbled through me. *Fuck yeah. This is a vehicle for zombie hunting*.

The driveway in front of us was clear. Men stood off to either side, guns ready in case those dead fuckers tried to get through while the gate was open. Of course, my dad was ready to shoot anything in front of us.

“Dad, if there are zombies in front of us?”

“Just run ’em over. This thing will take it.”

Right.

Time to go. I put my foot down gently, and we rolled forward. A little more, and it was about as fast as I dare to go.

I could see shadows beyond the gate. Zombies. The activity alone was attracting them.

I approached the gate. It started to roll open. “Lights?” I asked.

“Turn ’em on.”

On they went. There was a fucking mob in front of us. The zombies were already starting to slip through the opening in the gate. Rifles on either side of us opened up, and then I heard a rapid wham, wham, wham sound. Whatever my dad had on the top of this thing, it was loud and effective. The zombies stepping through the opening practically exploded, heads, guts, blood, all of it flying everywhere.

It didn’t look good, though. Where the fuck had they all come from? There weren’t that many when I raced through, earlier.

The gate stopped, about half way open. Too

many zombies were pressing on it in their efforts to get at the live bait. I couldn't just drive through it.

"What are we going to do?" I asked, trying not to sound panicked.

Over the wham, wham of his weapon, I don't think my dad heard me. He just kept mowing them down as the fuckers came through. The pieces piled up.

Chuck had his men direct their fire through the gate. I really started to wonder. Was my dad's whole neighborhood filled with ex-military?

The zombies fell away from the gate for a minute, and it resumed rolling.

And when it opened wide enough for the Humvee, as I gauged it, I stomped on the gas and drove the thing through and over the mass of dead flesh, clearing the way. The dead mostly went under us. Their bodies bounced us around as we rolled over them.

And then we were through the gate.

"Hold up!" my dad yelled.

I stepped on the brake and looked in the mirror. The gate was closing. A couple men cleared zombie parts from its track.

Wham, wham, wham. My dad took out a few remaining zombies.

I looked forward, and saw another wave running toward us.

"Dad?"

"Go!"

I floored it and the Humvee lurched forward. I ran right over those fuckers. My dad put lead into as many as he could. I really needed some ear protection.

I turned the corner, avoiding my dead car and its fading headlights, and drove through the newly empty neighborhood streets. We were on our way.

The drive back across the freeway scared me. The abandoned cars were still there, and the overpass was still free of zombies, but Alderwood Mall was now burning, a huge orange-red ball of fire in the distance. On the freeway below us, the zombies had filtered away, their prey either eaten, run away, or become zombies themselves. I-5 had become a graveyard of dead cars with fading headlights.

"Holy shit," my dad said as he took it all in. "I wonder how far this goes."

"At least all the way through Lynnwood," I said. "I tried to cross under on 44th, and I couldn't even get *to* the freeway."

"So, this Andrea girl. How long have you been seeing her?"

Something had happened to my dad. He'd never been interested in this kind of shit before.

"About a year."

"Serious?"

"What's it matter, anymore?" I asked. "Why are you even interested?"

"When your mom and I married, I was a different person. Then the Gulf War happened. I saw some shit I never had thought to see in my life."

"You were in the military, though." I said, choosing to accept the story as true.

"It was different, before. I never thought I'd actually have to go. Anyway, I came back, and I was just different. I knew it. Angry. Seemingly paranoid. Your mom chose to believe it never happened. I know she told you that my stories were just stories. I didn't love your mom any less, but eventually, we just couldn't be together."

"So, what's this have to do with Andrea?"

"Stress changes people," he said. "This shit is some serious stress. Don't be surprised if she changes on you, or you change on her."

I couldn't imagine myself changing, but I knew what he was trying to say. This zombie shit is really fucked up. What was true yesterday wasn't true anymore. Hell, I never even knew Andrea had a gun.

And my dad? My dad seemed to be changing right in front of me.

The rest of the trip, we spent in relative silence. Relative because the motor was fucking loud. We passed stalled vehicles, worked our way around makeshift roadblocks, and rolled over the top of a couple dozen zombies.

"We're almost there," I said, as we passed the 7-Eleven that served as the quickie beer run spot for about a dozen different apartment complexes in the area. Its windows were all shattered, the lights off.

"Turn the lights off," my dad said.

I slowed down and did as he said. The world outside went black.

"I wish I had some IR goggles or something that I could see through."

My dad laughed. "They don't work on these fuckers. No body heat at all. Just drive slow. Your night vision will return in a moment."

"What's the plan?"

"We'll pull up, get a look at the place, pull out, and make a plan. We need to see how many of those assholes are hanging around."

"Right."

A minute later, I eased up on the entrance to her apartment complex. "Just drive past it, slow and easy."

The apartment complex was dark, just like everything else.

My dad popped up out of the hole in the roof, and then played a spotlight right into the eyes of a zombie that had turned to look at the noise. He worked it around the parking lot, and I had to deliberately slow my breathing. A couple hundred zombies milled around in the parking lot. My dad moved the light up to the stair wells. Zombies packed every one of them. Andrea still had at least a few live neighbors.

"Keep driving," he said.

I stepped on the gas and we drove off.

“Does this road have a spot where we can turn around?” he asked.

“Not really, but it does loop around the complex.”

“That’ll work. Drive around, and just as we’re going to approach the entrance, slow down again. I want to thin them out before we go in. I’ve always wanted to try a drive by shooting.”

I did just as he said, and as we approached, the spotlight went on, and then I heard the wham, wham, wham of that big-ass gun.

The zombies were turning our way, those that hadn’t exploded into shredded body parts. I stepped on the gas.

The gun stopped for a second. “No, Brad. Slow down. Let them follow us.”

I slowed to ten miles an hour. Just about the speed those things could run. The gun picked back up again.

My phone rang. I only heard it because of a slight pause in my dad’s shooting. I picked it up and held it to my ear.

“Brad, there’s...my...”

“I can’t here you!” I yelled into the phone.

"...shooting outside..."

I wish I could turn that fucking gun down. I'd ask my dad to stop, but I didn't really want to be eaten by zombies.

"That's us," I yelled. "We're trying to clear the parking lot."

A zombie came out of the dark and I ran over it. It made the Humvee lurch a bit, mostly because it surprised me. I dropped the phone.

"Watch it!" My dad yelled.

"Sorry, zombie! Andrea's on the phone!"

"Call her back in a minute." The gun picked back up.

I found the cell by its LCD light and picked it back up. "I'll call you in a minute!" I said. I couldn't hear if she answered, so I closed the phone.

My dad ducked back inside.

"Right," he said. "So when we come around again, they're going to be in front of us. Turn on the lights as we pass, and this time, don't slow down. Run over any of the assholes that I don't manage to shoot."

"I can do that." This was beginning to sound like fun. "Do you think we'll get them all?"

"I doubt it. I think I got thirty or forty of 'em, that time around, but there are probably a couple hundred left. They won't all come out, either, I suspect."

"We've got another problem, too. We can't just pick up Andrea and leave the other survivors there, but clearing those stairwells is not a two man job, and I can't shoot up there for fear of hitting people."

I felt like he was telling me we couldn't even get Andrea.

"So what are you saying?"

"I'm open to ideas."

Great. My dad's the fucking military man, and he can't figure this out.

I could see the busted up 7-Eleven again in the distance. "We're coming up on the turn again."

He climbed back to his gun. "Well, let's see what we can do about the infestation, at least. Maybe we'll think of something."

I flicked the lights on and about a hundred yards in front of us, the zombies filled the road, milling around, confused as hell. Until, of course, the lights came on. They rushed us, and my dad opened up with the gun.

It seemed like a video game, to be honest. The lights gave the whole thing this eerie look as the zombies fell down in our path. My dad was good. Only a few got inside his range, but I ran them over with little trouble. I didn't doubt that they'd get back up, but we'd get them the next time around. I started to feel good about our chances, even with all the bouncing about as I drove over zombie remains.

Once we passed through, and the shooting stopped, I expected to see my dad again, but he stayed where he was.

"What now?" I yelled back to him.

"Next time around, drive into the parking lot."

My phone rang again.

"What are you doing?" she asked.

"We're driving around again, and then we're coming into the parking lot."

"I went out to my balcony and looked over. There aren't that many down there anymore."

Balcony. An idea, perhaps. "What about your stairwell?"

"They're still pounding at my door."

"Damn," I said.

"What?"

The 7-Eleven was in my sight again. "Go out to the balcony, Hun. Be ready."

"For what?"

"I don't know, I have an idea, but... just be ready."

"Okay," she said.

"Oh, one last thing," I said as I turned the corner.

"What?"

"Will you marry me?" I asked.

Silence from her for a moment. I knew I had surprised her.

The headlights were still on. I could see about a dozen zombies up and walking around on the road.

"I..." The gun cut her off, and I didn't hear her answer.

Fuck.

I slipped the phone into my pocket and prepared to get my girl, even if she said no.

I made the turn into the parking lot, and stopped. The headlights and my dad's spotlight illuminated the task we had ahead of us.

We had cleared the place pretty good, but there were still enough zombies about that we wouldn't be able to leave the Humvee without risking quick dismemberment.

I looked up at the third row apartments where I knew Andrea lived. Her balcony, and the balconies of the rest of the apartments hung out on the pavement side of the apartments. In between us and the balconies, besides a lot of zombies, were a row of carports. Most of the cars were gone. I bet they were out on I-5.

"Dad," I yelled. "I have an idea."

"What is it?"

"If she jumped from her balcony, do you think you could catch her?"

"You can't get this thing close enough," he said.

"I can try," I said.

I hit the gas and we started forward. The gun spoke again, clearing us a path through the remaining zombies. I aimed right for the carport that was out front of Andrea's balcony. Fortunately, the cars were gone.

At the last moment, my dad ducked down into Humvee and braced himself.

I drove right under the carport and up into the porch area of the bottom apartment directly beneath Andrea's. The collision jolted me forward, but I managed to hit the brake before we went too far.

"Fuck, Brad," my dad said as he went up top. I heard him yell, "Jump."

Dust swirled up in front of the lights, and I could see into the apartment in front of us. Two zombies were inside, bent over, chewing on something. One of them looked up, its white eyes glaring in the light.

I heard a thump on top of the Humvee, and then some scrabbling around.

The two zombies stood up.

"I'm in," Andrea said from behind me.

"Go, Brad, go!"

I threw it in reverse and backed up out of there, with the zombies following the lights. The remains of the fence I'd run through came with us.

A couple bumps and we were free.

I put it in drive and spun the wheel. Some gas, and we were driving through the parking lot. The wham, wham of the gun picked up again. I was beginning to get used to that noise.

I felt a hand on my shoulder, and then Andrea

plopped into the passenger seat. Dressed in black, like always, only this time, boots instead of heels, and a gun at her hip. Her hair, a bleach-blonde color, was tied back in a ponytail.

The gun stopped for a moment and my dad dropped his head in to issue some instructions. "Take it back up to the entrance. I want to see what we're looking at."

I did as I was told, running down a few zombies in the process. I would have never thought life could turn into a video game.

When we got to the entrance, I got us turned around. There weren't many zombies left in the parking lot, but they were moving toward us. My dad took out a few of them, then shined the spotlight at the balconies along the top floor of the building.

"Thanks for coming to get me," Andrea said while it was quiet. "If you weren't so far away, I'd kiss you."

I turned away from the carnage we'd created to look at her for a moment. Across the gulf that separated us—there must have been two or three feet of crap in between—I caught a smile cross her face. "How could I not?" I asked.

She laughed. Whatever panic I'd thought I'd heard in her voice over the phone was gone. "I thought I was the psycho one in this relationship."

"For the record, I never really thought you were psycho."

"I didn't pick the handle for nothing," she said.

My dad ducked inside. "All right, kids. I see four more people we might be able to save, which is good, since we don't have a whole lot of extra room in here. Look where the spotlight is pointing."

I looked. A woman and a kid. I couldn't really guess how old the kid was from here, but it was just over half the woman's height. They were waving their arms at us.

"Two of them?"

"Yes, we'll get them first."

In front of us, another wave of zombies approached in their half jog. "Time to go," I said.

The gun spit fire again, and the first row fell over. I stomped on the accelerator and ran us right through and over the rest.

I sped up, aimed us at another first floor fenced patio, and slipped the Humvee right under the carport again, smashing the wooden fence to pieces. This time, the apartment in front of me was empty.

I heard my dad yelling up at the woman. "Throw the kid, I'll catch him."

I heard a scream, then a thump as my dad caught the kid. The kid slipped down inside. I could hear him crying.

Andrea turned around and looked at him. "Pick a seat and buckle up," she said. "Your safe now."

I can only guess that the kid listened. I looked out my side window. A pair of zombies were running right at it, not three feet away.

I flinched back, expecting the glass to shatter, and screamed. I don't even remember if it was a girl scream this time. Heck, it might have even been the woman screaming as she jumped from her balcony.

The zombies slammed into the side of the Humvee with a thud, their hands hit the glass, and the window acquired a coating of zombie juices.

Andrea laughed.

The zombies kept trying to get in, pushing and pushing. I could feel the Humvee rock underneath me, but it wasn't going anywhere, and they weren't getting in.

The woman slid into the Humvee past my dad, and took the other empty seat.

My dad ducked in after her. "Armored windows, Brad," he said, and laughed. "Come on, back this thing out. Two more to get."

Right.

I put the beast in reverse, and we were out. The zombies slid off and started chasing us. Too close for my dad to hit.

Andrea pulled out her gun and slid her window open. "Put them on my side," she said.

I glanced at her real quick. She wasn't the girl I had thought I was proposing to. Maybe dad was right.

I heaved the wheel over so that she had a shot at them.

She stuck her gun out. Bang. Brain matter splattered out the back of the first one. Before it fell to the ground, bang, the second was on its way, too.

My dad laughed again. I'm not sure if he was starting to go fucking crazy, or if he actually found the whole situation humorous.

"Great shots," he said in between guffaws.

I had to agree. I guess if there had to be a woman that you'd want to marry after the zombie apocalypse, Andrea would be among the top finishers.

Of course, I still didn't know her answer.

"Where are the others?" I yelled back. Two more to go.

"The first is two apartments down."

Right. First a tight left, as tight as I could in this thing, and then a turn to the right and I ran us right under and through another fence. I was getting good at crushing fences. I put it in reverse as soon as we came to a stop, ready to pull out.

The first thing that went wrong was an unlucky blow to a headlamp. A post from the shattered fence slipped through the bars on the front of the Humvee and pierced it. We still had one working headlamp, though.

The second thing to go wrong was the apartment in front of us. Zombie party. I couldn't count all the zombies inside, but there were enough that I knew we were in serious trouble, especially since the patio doors had already shattered. If they saw my dad up there, they'd just climb onto the hood and right up to him.

"Dad, hurry! We can't stay."

The kid behind me was starting to cry again, or maybe he was still crying. I couldn't blame him, really. The fuckers scared the shit out of me, too.

I heard my dad exhorting the person we were trying to rescue to jump. I don't know what the problem was, but they were sure taking their time getting down.

"Brad," Andrea said.

She didn't have to say anything. I could see it already. The zombies in front of us had finally figured out we were food, I think, and started to run for us. "Dad!"

And then I heard a thump on the roof.

For a moment, I thought our target had jumped, until I heard my dad scream.

Zombies started to climb up onto the hood. Andrea stuck her arm out and fired. One went down. Another shot, and another went down.

The roof thumped again.

"Go, go!" I heard my dad yell, and then shots from him, but not the big gun.

Fuck. That was the third thing to go wrong. I hit the gas, and we went backward quickly. Another shot from Andrea cleared a second zombie from the hood, but it was replaced by a zombie that rolled down from the roof.

"Oh shit!" I yelled.

Another zombie fell onto the hood from above us. The second floor balcony. I put my foot into the accelerator, while watching the zombies on top of us, and not paying attention to what was behind us.

Andrea shot again, but missed this time.

My head slammed into the headrest behind me as the Humvee came to a sudden stop. Lights flashed through my brain for a moment.

A second passed, maybe two, before I realized what had happened. The zombies had fallen off in the collision, but they were already up again, assaulting the sides of the Humvee.

"Everybody alright?" I asked.

I wasn't too worried about our zombies

outside, though more were piling out of the apartment we'd just vacated.

I heard assents from everybody except my dad.

"Brad, your dad," said Andrea. She had already turned to look backward.

I poked my head around my seat to find my dad hanging limply in his harness.

Anger ripped through me. I wanted to shoot the fucker who wouldn't jump, who caused my dad to get hurt or die. If it weren't for that asshole...

"Get us out of here," Andrea said. "I'll take care of your dad."

Then the other woman spoke up. "You stay there, miss. I'm a nurse. I'll help him."

I put it in drive and drove away from those zombies. I ran over a half dozen others, which made me feel better.

"Try not to jostle us so much," said the nurse. "Your dad is bleeding. A cut on his forehead, I think, but he's still alive."

Okay, just knocked out. I could deal with that.

What I couldn't deal with was what to do next. My dad had said there was at least one more we could rescue. We weren't going back after that asshole that didn't jump. Too many zombies there, for one, and two, he didn't deserve to be rescued. Not by me.

But the other, I think my dad would have wanted me to try.

"Can you get him down from there?"

I was coming up on the end of the parking lot. I'd have to turn around.

I executed a three point turn using a couple of empty parking spaces, and found myself looking head on at about fifteen zombies running toward us.

I heard a thump in the cabin behind us. "He's down."

Andrea didn't even wait for me to ask her to climb up in the turret before she was unbuckling herself.

"Hurry up," I said. They're almost on us.

"I'm hurrying."

She did, too. I mentally marked the distance between us and the zombies. Thirty feet... Twenty feet... Ten feet...

"I'm in," she yelled.

I sent the Humvee rolling through them, knocking them to the side or just running over them.

Wham. The gun went off again, and I heard Andrea whoop with joy. I smiled, even with the stress of everything going on, it was good to hear Andrea enjoying herself.

When we broke through the wave, and the gun had stopped, I called up to her. “My dad had a spotlight up there. Can you use it to find the last stranded person he was talking about?”

I saw the light sweep the balconies. One after another, they were empty. Where was he?

The light played over one last balcony. There he was, one leg already over the railing.

“I see him,” I yelled to Andrea. “He’ll have to jump to the hood. I’m not risking the last headlamp.” We’d need it to get back to my dad’s place.

“Right.”

More careful this time, I drove right up to the first floor patio, but not through its fence. It’s a good thing I stopped when I did. The guy didn’t wait for me to stop before he dropped to the hood. He landed awkwardly on one ankle, and I swear I could hear it snap through the armored window.

He cried out in pain, but he didn’t waste any

time climbing up to the turret area, despite the broken ankle. He told me later that he was seriously terrified we'd leave him.

I backed out, whipped around as fast as the Humvee would let me, and drove our asses out of the apartment complex.

I glanced back to look at my dad, but in the dark, I couldn't see him. For the first time in years, I felt like I'd made a connection with him, and I couldn't stomach the thought of losing him so soon after losing my mom.

5

I turned off the light as we rolled around the corner, past my broken piece of shit car. I stopped there for a minute to let my eyes adjust. I didn't think we were dragging any zombies behind us, but I didn't want to attract the roaming shitbags to the gate while we waited for it to open. I could hear the moans in the back.

"How are they," I asked the nurse while I waited to see again.

"Your dad is still out. The other..."

"Sean," the guy said in between moans.

I couldn't tell for sure in the darkness, but when she continued, I thought she sounded annoyed at being interrupted. "Okay, Sean is in real pain because of his ankle."

So the moans weren't from my dad.

"Why is the house so dark?" Andrea asked.

"Blackout windows."

When my eyes finally adjusted and I could see my dad's fence from where we sat, something looked wrong. I expected to see people in the yard, but it looked empty and lifeless.

"Can you see anyone in the yard? There ought to be someone on watch."

"I can't see anyone."

I pulled out my phone and dialed my dad's number. The phone in his fucking pocket rang. Of course he hadn't given me his home number. He didn't want Alicia to take my calls. Not that I'd called him before this.

"Get that phone," I said.

When my dad's ring was unmuffled, I ended the call. His phone kept ringing.

"Fuck!" I remembered that Alicia would call him if something went wrong. "Give it to me."

When the hunk of plastic was in my hand, I answered it.

"Hello?"

"Bill?" Alicia's voice, unsure and frightened. I

had little trouble imagining what might have caused her to sound that way.

"No, it's Brad. Dad's hurt."

"He's not bit, is he?"

"No, cut on his head." I hoped that's all it was.

She sighed through the phone. "Brad, don't come back. Just go somewhere else, find a safe zone, go camp in the mountains, but don't come back."

"Why?"

"Somehow, they got in. Someone was bit, a break in the perimeter, someone let them in, I don't know. I'm down in the basement. There are four of us here. We've got food to last the month, at least, but there's no way we're getting out right now, and there are far too many of them in the house above us. You'll never make it."

"Only four? Where are the others?"

"Dead or infected, or whatever you might call it."

"You're sure you're safe?"

"As safe as anyone. This basement is a bomb shelter. Nothing's getting in that we don't let in."

I thought about it for a long time. I pondered turning the lights on, drawing them out, shooting the fuckers down, but we'd already used lots of ammo. I had no idea how much was left, and Alicia said they were safe. And while I'd just become the worlds best zombie mower with this Humvee, there were other considerations. We had four people in the back that were essentially useless in a fight, and once inside the house, we'd have to get out and fight.

"Alright," I said, "We'll be back in three weeks to get you out. Sooner, if possible."

"Okay. Tell your dad I love him, will ya? I know you and I never really got along, but..."

"Don't worry about it," I said. "I think I understand now."

I didn't think I was lying to her, either.

"You take care of him for me," she said.

"I will." This was going to be one of those conversations where no one wanted to hang up. Fuck that. "I've gotta go," I said.

"Right. Take care." Then she hung up.

I turned his phone off to conserve the battery, and wondered while doing it if the voice-mail worked. I reversed past my car, turned on our headlamp, and saw zombies flood out of my dad's house and the surrounding homes that lined the street. I spun the wheel and drove us out of there, away from the safety I had thought existed there.

"Where are we going," Andrea asked.

"Come down here," I said.

Seconds later, she sat in the seat across from me, and I told her what had happened.

"That still doesn't tell me where we're going," she said.

"Some place safe, I hope. We'll need to get fuel soon. This thing eats a lot of it." The gauge said a quarter of a tank. I hoped I could believe it. "We also need to find some medical supplies—a pharmacy or something—for my dad and Sean."

"Right."

"And any place we go needs to be out of the way. You saw the mall."

"Zombie movies didn't exactly prepare us for the zombie apocalypse, did they?"

I laughed. "I've been having those same thoughts."

"What place is out of the way, yet has enough supplies nearby to survive on?"

"My first thought was eastern Washington.

Somewhere small where there just aren't a lot of people, but I think the passes over the mountains will be impassable. From where we're at, there are only two alternatives—Highway 2 over Stevens and the North Cascades Highway."

"That's a long way to go in this thing," Andrea said.

"I know. The other option I can think of is heading down to the waterfront and finding a boat to take us out into the San Juans, but I don't know anything about boats except that they float."

"Remember the credits in the remake of *Dawn of the Dead*?"

"Yeah, that frightens me, too. I thought they should have left that part out. It ruined the movie for me."

We fell silent. I drove us back over I-5, and then turned right along the freeway.

We needed to get away from civilization while we were still trapped on the west side of the mountains. Going south through the built up areas was a suicide run, I thought. What we needed was a bunker with sight-lines that would let us see those fuckers coming from a mile away. Fences that would keep them out. Nearby supplies that wouldn't all be used up and looted.

"There's farmland up north around Mt. Vernon and Burlington," I said.

She looked at me. I couldn't get a read on her expression in the dim lights of the dashboard. "We could board up the lower floor windows on a farmhouse, if we can find one that's empty."

"As long as we don't get shot first."

I nodded. "We'd have to be careful, but there aren't nearly as many people up there."

"How do we get there? I-5's a mess."

"Highway 9. It runs all the way to Canada, and bypasses all of the large cities. I think it's our best chance."

She put her hand out on the hump that kept us separated, and I reached out and took hold of it. Her hand was warm, her skin soft. I could only hold it for a moment, though. The Humvee wasn't meant for one handed driving.

"First, we need to find a gas station," I said after looking at the fuel gauge and finding it near empty. I knew Humvees were gas hogs, but damn. I wondered if this thing would even get a hundred miles on a tank.

The closest station actually sat on Filbert Road, my planned route to Highway 9. My worry was that it stood damned square in the midst of a thousand homes, but the alternatives were farther away and less accessible.

"There's a 7-Eleven up here on Filbert," Andrea said, echoing my thoughts.

"Yeah, I know. Why don't you get back in the turret. We're almost there. I just hope there's power to pump the gas." Don't say anything. I know the fucker runs on diesel.

She climbed back and stuck her head out the top again. I would have liked to watch her, but I had to keep my eyes on the road. I didn't want to drive us into the ditch or collide with an overturned vehicle.

When we were almost to the 7-Eleven, the most miraculous thing to happen—other than the dead returning to life—happened. I started to see signs of power in the buildings around us. A porch light, a room light.

And when we pulled up to the 7-Eleven, it was

lit up like some sort of beacon to us weary travelers. I just hoped it wasn't a fucking beacon to the zombies. I was surprised, really, that I didn't see any around.

The glass at the front of the store had been smashed. I don't know if zombies had done that, or if looters had. I laughed when I realized that I would feel safer if zombies smashed it. Zombies don't shoot people.

I pulled up next to the diesel pump and shut the thing down.

The quiet was eerie.

"You see anything, Andrea?" I asked.

"Nothing. It doesn't mean they aren't out there, but I would have expected zombies would be rushing us right now if they were around."

"I bet they're all in among the homes," I said. The thought didn't make me feel any better.

I turned to look at the nurse. Light from outside shone through the windows, and I could see her for the first time. If I'd had to guess, she was in her late thirties. The stress of the day had engraved itself on her face. Her eyes were big and wide, but her movements hinted at someone who could control herself amidst some really shitty situations. My guess is that she'd worked in the E.R.

"What's your name?" I asked.

"Sarah."

What were the chances of meeting two Sarahs in one night? I don't know if it meant anything, but I was pretty sure the other one was already dead. "Right," I said. "How's my dad?"

Andrea climbed down out of the harness.

Sarah looked at him. "He's sweating, but his skin is cold. We need to get him a blanket and bandages. I've tried to do what I could, but it keeps bleeding through." I saw she had ripped up some of her shirt and tied it around my dad's head. It didn't seem to be doing the job. His face was covered in blood.

Andrea found my dad's gun stash. She picked one up, hefted it, then handed it to me. A shotgun with a Tommy-gun like magazine. She picked up another one, and this one she kept for herself.

"Hey kid," she said, "What's your name?"

"Danny."

I looked at the kid for the first time, too. He

had a shock of blonde hair, thick, atop his head. He was nine or ten, at a guess. Crazy thing, too. His name, same as that of my next door neighbor. First Sarah, then him. Night of the living names or something.

"Danny, my name is Andrea, and this is Brad," Andrea said. "Can you climb up there and be a lookout for us? Look all around, and if you see a zombie, yell out."

He nodded.

"Are you sure that's a good idea?" I asked.

"He'll be safe up there, as long as he doesn't touch anything."

"I won't touch anything," the kid said. He started scrambling up, climbing the harness as much as climbing into it. It was far too big for him. He'd probably just have to sit up there.

"Why aren't you..."

"Because I'm going to go authorize the pump from inside and look for a blanket and bandages while you fill the tank. Sarah needs to watch our wounded, and I don't think she wants to be far from Danny."

I could see her point. Sean was useless, too.

His ankle wouldn't let him do anything. Getting him in the harness would be a chore, and I didn't think we had the time to wrestle with that. I felt it ticking away.

"Let's go then," I said.

Andrea smiled, then opened the side door.

I opened my door, climbed down, then reached in and grabbed the rapier. I wasn't going to go out with just the shotgun.

"What's the sword for?" she asked.

"Just in case," I said. "I can't hit a barn with a gun."

"That's why I gave you the shotgun," she said, laughing. "If they're close enough, you almost don't have to aim."

I kept the sword anyway. I knew I could kill zombies with it.

"Just get going," I said, and then I did something impulsive. I reached out and pulled her close to me. "Be careful," I said, and then kissed her.

Her lips felt warm, soft. I had missed them, even though it had been only a day since I'd last kissed them.

She pulled away. “Let’s make this quick,” she said, and then ran across the parking lot, gun held ready to aim and fire. I wondered for a moment if she’d been in the military and hadn’t told me. It would’t surprise me. She kept much of her earlier life a secret. I’d always assumed it was some horror show of a family behind her reticence to talk about her past, but for the first time, I realized there might be other reasons to keep quiet. Who the hell had I asked to marry?

And why did she sound so panicky on the phone, but since we rescued her, she was all business and kick ass. Was the panic an act?

I stood and watched her for a moment before I shook off those worries. They weren’t important. Surviving was important.

I opened the fuel cap on the Humvee, then took the nozzle from the diesel pump and plunged it into the opening.

I called up to the kid. “You see anything, Danny?”

“No,” he said. His voice was a bit quiet.

“Make sure you yell if you do.”

Andrea was in the 7-Eleven, and behind the

counter already, looking over something. She reached out and touched a button, and the pump came on.

Fuck yeah. I squeezed the handle, flipped that little lever down to keep it pumping, and then started walking around the Humvee. Sure the kid was up top, but I didn't exactly trust my life to a ten-year-old.

I made a trip around once, and it was still pumping fuel.

I heard a noise at the door of the Humvee, and it opened. Sarah stuck her head out.

"Your dad is moving. I think he's waking up."

I ran to the door and looked in. The interior was still plenty dark, but I could see the fingers on his hand twitching like he was dreaming.

My body wanted to jump up and down. My dad was going to be all right. He'd live, and we'd go back and save Alicia, and maybe I could have a real family for the first time in several years.

"Andrea," I yelled. "Hurry! My dad's waking up!"

My dad's fingers flexed themselves, then formed a fist. They extended again. He really was waking up.

His arm came up slowly, so slowly, and his wrist moved through a beam of light that snuck past me, and his sleeve slipped down just enough to reveal a ring of red welts and broken skin.

"Shit!"

"Shit, shit!"

"Sarah, get out! Get the fuck out of there."

I reached for her arm to try to pull on her, but I was late. My dad's arm went from moving slowly to moving rapidly in the space of a heartbeat, and clutched at her.

He sat up, his other arm latched on, and pulled Sarah down to him.

I dropped the shotgun. I couldn't use it in the Humvee.

Danny screamed the high pitch squeal that only a kid not gone through puberty can achieve. Sean made his own terror filled sounds.

"Fuck–fuck! Andrea!"

I drew the rapier, but I couldn't reach my dad around Sarah.

I ran around the other side of the Humvee, and caught sight of Andrea running full bore, weapon drawn, toward me.

"What's going on?" she asked.

"My dad's a fucking zombie!" I yelled.

I yanked the door open. I knew it was too late to save Sarah, but Sean was still back there, still alive.

My dad didn't even look at me. He had his head buried in Sarah's throat, tearing at it with his teeth.

I stabbed with the rapier, right into his neck. It didn't slow him down, and when he twisted to see what had struck him, the strength of his movement ripped the sword from my hand.

My dad, the zombie, dropped Sarah and began pulling himself through the door toward me.

I backed up, weaponless. Why the fuck did I drop the shotgun?

"Andrea?" I called out.

My zombie dad fell out of the car, and then stood up. He looked at me, tilted his head to the side as if pondering what I was. I wondered for a moment if he still knew me, if there was still something of my dad left inside.

Danny continued to scream atop the Humvee, only now, he called out to his mom. "Mommy! Mommy!" Every word was punctuated by a sob.

My dad took a step forward, then another step.

I wished I had a gun. I wished I knew how to use one. I would have shot my dad right in the head if I could have. I'm not one of those dumb fucks in the movies who thinks their loved one is still inside that zombie, hiding out, waiting for the right moment to emerge.

The tilt of his head corrected itself as he took another step, and then another.

His arms came up, and he surged forward.

Blam. His head exploded, a bullet smashing into it from the side. There was little left of it atop his torso once the bullet did its job.

My dad's body fell to the ground, lifeless, like a dead body should.

I heard the click from the fuel pump. The tank was full.

Danny turned out to be a fairly resilient little kid. I kind of liked him. He cried about his mom for quite a while after we pulled her from the Humvee and laid her down on the ground. She wasn't moving, and we all knew she would come back to some fucked up afterlife soon.

None of us really had the heart to end it for her in front of Danny, but Danny surprised us all. In a calm moment as we sat in the Humvee looking at her, in between sobs, he said, "She's going to turn into a zombie, isn't she?"

"Probably," Andrea said. Her voice was calm, soothing, almost motherly. The kind of voice I imagined my mom would have used.

"Then we have to stop it. I don't think she'd like being a zombie."

"Are you sure?"

He nodded.

Andrea got out of the Humvee carrying her pistol. Danny got out with her, and the two of them went to stand near her head.

Danny put his arms around Andrea, and I saw Andrea's lips move, but I couldn't hear her words.

When she was done speaking, she drew her gun, and fired a single bullet into Sarah's temple.

It set Danny to crying again, but he didn't leave Andrea's side, and once they climbed back in, we left the 7-Eleven and headed, hopefully, for a safer place.

Once Danny had quieted down and seemed to be sleeping and Sean was snoring away in the back, Andrea came to sit next to me, and I decided I had to ask.

I put my hand out on the hump between us, and she took it. A good sign, I thought.

"When I asked you to marry me over the phone, I didn't hear your answer," I said.

She squeezed my hand, and smiled.

"I said yes, but I don't think I was in my right mind at that moment," she said.

My heart sank. "So the answer is no?"

"The answer is yes, but there is one condition."

"What's that?" I asked.

She laughed. "You need to learn how to shoot."

I laughed, too. For her, I'll learn anything.

About The Author

Mark Fassett lives in western Washington with his wife, children, and cats. He's had extensive experience in the mobile game business and was involved with some of the top selling titles at the time of their release, including multiple Duke Nukem Mobile games and Guitar Hero World Tour Mobile. He's also played and written music most of his life, and was "this close" to actually making money at it.

Find Me Online

Blog - http://www.markfassett.com
Twitter - http://twitter.com/mark_fassett

Zombies Ate My Mom! was written using StoryBox. StoryBox is software I developed specifically for writing fiction. You can try it for free at http://www.storyboxsoftware.com

Made in the USA
Charleston, SC
04 April 2012